★ GET A HOLD ★
OF YOUR ELF!

★ Also in the ★
MS. FROGBOTTOM'S FIELD TRIPS series

MS. FROGBOTTOM'S FIELD TRIPS

★ GET A HOLD OF YOUR ELF! ★

By **AIDEN**, *as told to* **NANCY KRULIK**
Illustrated by **HARRY BRIGGS**

ALADDIN
New York London Toronto Sydney New Delhi

For Jeff and Amy

—N. K.

ALADDIN
An imprint of Simon & Schuster Children's Publishing Division
1230 Avenue of the Americas, New York, New York 10020
First Aladdin paperback edition September 2021
Text copyright © 2021 by Nancy Krulik
Illustrations copyright © 2021 by Harry Briggs
Also available in an Aladdin hardcover edition.
All rights reserved, including the right of reproduction in whole or in part in any form.
ALADDIN and related logo are registered trademarks of Simon & Schuster, Inc.
For information about special discounts for bulk purchases, please contact
Simon & Schuster Special Sales at 1-866-506-1949 or business@simonandschuster.com.
The Simon & Schuster Speakers Bureau can bring authors to your live event.
For more information or to book an event contact the Simon & Schuster Speakers
Bureau at 1-866-248-3049 or visit our website at www.simonspeakers.com.
Cover designed by Karin Paprocki
Interior designed by Mike Rosamilia
The illustrations for this book were rendered digitally.
The text of this book was set in Neutraface Slab Text.
Manufactured in the United States of America 0821 OFF
2 4 6 8 10 9 7 5 3 1
Library of Congress Control Number 2021932949
ISBN 9781534454064 (hc)
ISBN 9781534454057 (pbk)
ISBN 9781534454071 (ebook)

WELCOME TO CLASS 4A.

We have a warning for you:

BEWARE OF THE MAP.

Our classroom probably looks a lot like yours. We have chairs, desks, a whiteboard, and artwork on the walls. And of course we have our teacher, Ms. Frogbottom.

Actually, our teacher is the reason why things sometimes get strange around here. Because Ms. Frogbottom is kind of *different*.

For starters, she carries around a backpack. It looks like any other pack, but somehow strange things always seem to be popping out of it. You don't have to worry about most of the stuff our teacher carries. But if she reaches into her pack and pulls out her giant map, beware. That map is *magic*. It has the power to lift us right out of our classroom and drop us in some faraway place. And somehow it's always the exact same time as when we left. No matter where we go, we wind up meeting frightening creatures none of us ever believed were real—and getting into all sorts of trouble.

You don't have to be *too* scared, though. Things always seem to turn out okay for us in the end. Or at least they have *so far.* . . .

Your new pals,

Aiden, Emma, Oliver, Olivia, Sofia, and Tony

MS. FROGBOTTOM'S
FiELD TRiP
DO'S aND DON'TS

- Do stay together.

- Don't take photos. You can't experience the big world through a tiny camera hole.

- Don't bring home souvenirs. We want to leave the places we visit exactly as we found them.

- Don't use the word "weird." The people, places, and food we experience are just different from what you are used to.

- Do have fun!

1

"I DON'T KNOW WHY WE'RE HAVING RECESS outside," Tony complains as our class stands together on the playground. "It's so cold, my eyeballs are gonna freeze."

"That can't happen," Sofia assures him. "The warm blood circulating through your body keeps your eyes from freezing over."

Tony blinks twice, like he's trying to make sure she's right. He shouldn't bother. Sofia's the class brain. She has a photographic memory, which means she can remember everything she's ever read.

But Tony's right too. It's really cold out here. Especially since we're just standing around.

"We'd feel warmer if we moved," I say. "Let's play tag. Oliver, you be it."

"Who made you king, Aiden?" Emma demands.

"What are you talking about?" I ask her.

"No one said we wanted to play tag," Emma begins.

"You run a lot in tag," I explain. "Running warms you up."

"He's right," Sofia says. "When your muscles move, they generate body heat."

Emma shrugs. "Fine, we'll play tag.

★ 6 ★

But why does Aiden get to say who's it?"

"Do *you* want to be it?" Oliver asks her.

"No," Emma answers. "I'm just saying it's not up to Aiden."

"What if I *want* to be it?" Oliver demands.

"Do you?" I ask him.

Oliver nods, covers his eyes, and starts counting backward. "Ten, nine, eight . . ."

We scatter.

". . . four, three, two, one," Oliver continues. "Ready or not, here I come!"

Oliver takes off, trying to tag one of us. I figure he'll go straight for Sofia. She's the slowest—mostly because she's always carrying her tablet around, taking care not to drop it.

Instead Oliver takes off in *my* direction.

Bad move, Oliver. I may be the shortest kid in Class 4A, but I'm also the fastest.

I dart up the hill. I can hear Oliver running behind me, but I don't dare turn, because that will slow me down.

I'm really moving now. Fast. Faster—

"Aiden! Watch out!" I hear Olivia shout. "That icicle over your head looks like it's gonna fall. It's really sharp."

I stop short and look at the oak branches. "I don't see any icicles," I tell Olivia.

"Tag!" Oliver says as he sneaks up and tags me. "You're it!"

"That's not fair!" I glare angrily at Olivia. "You cheated to help your brother."

"I could've sworn I saw an icicle up

there." Olivia starts giggling, which lets me know she's lying.

"That tag doesn't count," I insist. "We have to start over."

"Says who?" Oliver argues.

"Says me," I reply.

"Aiden is acting like the boss." Emma comes running up the hill. *"Again."*

"Butt out, Emma," I tell her. "This isn't your business."

"Sure it is," she says. "We're all playing this game."

"We're not playing anything," Sofia points out as she and Tony walk over. "We're just arguing."

She's right. But that's not *my* fault.

"See what you did?" I ask Olivia.

"You got us all mad at each other."

"I did not," Olivia says. "I just said I thought I saw an icicle."

"You didn't say you *thought*," I remind her.

"I'm still freezing." Tony wraps his arms around his chest. "Let's ask Ms. Frogbottom if we can go inside."

"I'm with Tony," Sofia says.

"Me too," Emma adds.

Oliver and Olivia both nod.

So much for playing tag.

"Hey, Tony," Olivia says as we walk

FROGBOTTOM FACT

★ Icicles form when snow or ice melts into small water drips, which are then refrozen by air temperatures that are below freezing (32 degrees Fahrenheit).

toward our teacher. "Do you want to learn how to speak another language?"

"Sure!" Tony replies. "What language?"

"It's called ... um ... Slobbotini," Olivia tells him.

Funny. I've never heard of that language.

Apparently neither has Sofia, because she says, "There's no such thing as Slob—"

"Repeat after me," Olivia tells Tony, talking really loudly to drown out Sofia. *"Awa."*

"Awa," Tony repeats.

"Tasee," Olivia continues.

"Tasee," Tony says after her.

"Leegoo," Olivia continues.

"Leegoo," Tony echoes.

"Siam," Olivia finishes.

"*Siam*," Tony says.

"Great!" Olivia cheers. "Now put it all together."

"*Awa tasee leegoo siam*," Tony says.

Olivia starts laughing. "You certainly are."

"Why? What does it mean?" Tony asks.

"You just said, 'Oh, what a silly goose I am,'" Emma tells Tony.

Tony turns beet red. "That's not funny."

"Sure it is." Olivia laughs so hard that she snorts.

"Ignore her," Oliver tells Tony. "She got a box of practical jokes from our aunt Maddie. That joke must be in the book that came with it."

"Are you ready to go inside?" Ms. Frogbottom asks from behind her giant scarf.

★ 13 ★

"Definitely," Emma tells her. "It's really cold out here."

"Okay." Ms. Frogbottom bends down to pick up her backpack. "Then let's— AAAAAHHHHH! MOUSE!"

Ms. Frogbottom jumps up in the air in fright.

Whoa. I've never seen our teacher scared before—which is saying something, considering the creepy characters our class has met up with on our field trips.

For instance, there was this mummy we met in Egypt who tried to trap us in his tomb of doom.

And there was a sea monster that whipped up a storm at Loch Ness in Scotland.

And don't even get me started about the time we met the Transylvanian vampire who was out for blood.

Strangely enough, after all that, it turns out that the one thing that scares Ms. Frogbottom is a mouse!

"Are you talking about *this*?" Olivia

picks the mouse up by the tail and dangles it in the air.

We all jump back.

Only, the mouse doesn't wiggle like you'd think it would. *Because it isn't a real mouse.* It's a stuffed toy.

"I can't believe you thought it was an actual mouse," Olivia says, giggling.

Olivia's got guts. It's one thing for her to play practical jokes on us. It's another for her to play them on our *teacher*.

"Olivia's in trouble," Tony whispers. "Ms. Frogbottom's gonna tell her they have to have a talk."

I know exactly what kind of "talk" Tony is referring to. I've had a few with Ms. Frogbottom. She sits you down and tells you how disappointed she is in you. It's awful.

I would feel bad for Olivia right now—if she hadn't been such a jerk to me while we were playing tag.

But Ms. Frogbottom doesn't tell Olivia that they'll be having a talk. Instead she *smiles*.

Huh?

"We have a practical joker," Ms. Frog-bottom says. "How fun. I'm sure Olivia would like to learn all about some cham-pion jokesters. I know just the place where she can do that."

Our teacher reaches into her backpack and pulls out a giant map. My friends and I look at one another nervously. We know what that map means.

We're going on a field trip. Right now. That map is our field trip transportation.

I know that sounds crazy, but it's the truth. Ms. Frogbottom's map is *magic*. All she has to do is touch a country, and . . . POW! The next thing we know, we're there.

"I wonder where we're going today?" Sofia asks.

"I hope it's someplace warm," Emma suggests. "Maybe with a beach."

"I don't care where we go," Tony declares. "As long as there are no monsters there."

I have a feeling Tony's not going to be happy. There are *always* creepy creatures lurking around on Ms. Frogbottom's field trips.

Our teacher points to a tiny island near the top of the map, right in the middle of the Atlantic Ocean.

"Here we go!" I shout as a white light flashes all around us. My body feels weightless, and I think my feet have just left the ground.

It's like I'm flying in space. And then . . .

I FEEL LIKE I'VE LANDED ON THE MOON.

I'm not kidding. When I was in second grade, I did a report about the moon, and the pictures I saw looked like this. The ground is rocky and dusty, and my boots leave deep prints—like the astronauts' boots left on the surface of the moon. There's a deep crater not far from where we're standing that looks a lot like the craters on the moon.

But I don't think we're on the moon.
We couldn't breathe if we were, because
there's no atmosphere up there. So I'm
sure we're somewhere on Earth.

FROGBOTTOM FACT

★ Iceland's landscape is so similar to that of the moon
  that Apollo astronauts actually trained for their
  moon mission in Iceland.

Ms. Frogbottom puts the Magic Map back into her pack and pulls out a strange hat. It's made of metal and has horns sticking out the sides.

"Now I feel like I fit in," our teacher says as she puts on the hat.

I can't imagine why wearing a hat with horns would make her fit in anywhere.

"Are those volcanoes?" Tony asks, pointing to some large mountains in the distance. They're wide at the bottom and narrow at the top.

Ms. Frogbottom nods. "This whole island is formed from the lava of erupting volcanoes."

"I thought volcanoes were only in Hawaii," I say.

"We're definitely *not* in Hawaii," Emma says as she pulls her hat down lower to cover her ears.

"No kidding." Sometimes I think Emma just says stuff to get on my nerves.

"There are volcanoes all over the world," Ms. Frogbottom tells me.

"Wherever we are, it's icy cold," Tony says, rubbing his mittens together. "We could use a nice, warm fire."

"Exactly right, Tony!" Ms. Frogbottom says excitedly. "We're in the land of fire and ice."

I think Ms. Frogbottom's brain may be frozen—although Sofia would probably tell me that that's impossible. "You can't have fire and ice in one place," I tell our teacher. "The fire would melt the ice."

"That's true," Ms. Frogbottom admits. "But this country is known for its areas of both fire and ice."

"The fire is the fiery lava that pours out of the volcanoes, right?" Emma asks.

Our teacher nods.

"And the ice is because it's so cold here?" Oliver wonders.

"Not exactly," Sofia says as she studies an article on her tablet. "That part of the nickname comes from the glaciers. There are more than two hundred and fifty of them here."

"Where's here?" I ask her.

"Iceland." Sofia sounds like she thinks I should have known that already. Which

I might have, if I carried a tablet around with me wherever I went, like she does.

"This country was discovered more than one thousand years ago by explorers from the Viking age," Sofia adds, smiling at Ms. Frogbottom. "That's why you're wearing a Viking helmet."

"Exactly!" Ms. Frogbottom cheers. "What a field trip this will be! We're going to see volcanoes, waterfalls, and lava tunnels. We may even take an outdoor bath in the geothermal springs. . . ."

Tony's eyes open wide. "An outdoor bath?" he asks nervously. "In this cold? In front of everyone?"

Olivia laughs. "Tony fell for another joke. You're kidding, right, Ms. Frogbottom?"

Our teacher shakes her head. "The water in geothermal lakes is heated by the earth's crust, so they're very warm. And we'll all be wearing bathing suits," she adds, smiling at Tony.

"But first we're going to see a huge waterfall," Ms. Frogbottom continues. "Actually, *two* waterfalls, with

two separate drops. The falls are called the Gullfoss."

As we follow my teacher, my eyes tear up from the crazy winds blowing into my face. I have to wrap my scarf around my mouth and nose just to be able to breathe. My hot breath makes my scarf all moist. My nose is starting to run,

FROGBOTTOM FACTS

★ "*Gullfoss*" means "golden falls." It was given that name because the water takes on a golden color in sunlight.

★ The water appears golden because it is glacial water that contains a large amount of golden-brown sediment that has been carved from the earth.

★ Gullfoss is part of Iceland's Golden Circle, a 186-mile route to the three most popular attractions in Iceland. In addition to Gullfoss, the Golden Circle includes the Geysir Geothermal Area in Haukadular Valley, and Thingvellir National Park.

right into the wool. It's all pretty gross.

In the distance I hear something that sounds like waves crashing, only a whole lot louder, and much more powerful. Unlike with waves, the crashing sound doesn't stop, not even for a second. It gets louder and louder as we get closer, until finally we can see the falls.

"Holy cow!" Oliver exclaims.

"Wow!" Emma adds.

"Remarkable!" Sofia says breathlessly.

The water in the falls has a golden tint that shimmers as the water rushes from the tops of the falls to the ground. The drop from both falls is very steep, and the water is showering endlessly down to the ground far below.

For what seems like a really long time, I stand there watching the water falling, feeling the wind whipping around me. Even though it's sunny out, the air feels damp because of the spray from the falls.

"Yikes!" I jump six feet in the air as someone—or some*thing*—taps me suddenly on the shoulder. I was staring at the falls so intently that I didn't notice anyone sneaking up behind me. My heart is pounding as I slowly turn around to see—

Phew. It's just Ms. Frogbottom. She's saying something to me, but I can't hear her over the sound of the water. I turn and follow her and the rest of my class back toward the road.

"Isn't it amazing how powerful that

water is?" Ms. Frogbottom says a few minutes later, when we're back walking on the road and we can hear her again. "The hard rock on top of the waterfalls is made of lava and—"

"Look at this cute little house!" Emma exclaims, interrupting our teacher.

Ms. Frogbottom shoots Emma a look.

Emma scrunches up her mouth and

looks down. "Sorry," she apologizes. She raises her hand.

"Yes, Emma?" Ms. Frogbottom asks.

"I was just noticing the tiny house by the side of the road." Emma points to what looks like a red-and-white dollhouse in the snow.

"That's an elf house," Ms. Frogbottom explains.

Olivia giggles. "Good one, Ms. Frogbottom," she says.

"I'm not kidding," Ms. Frogbottom replies. "Many people in Iceland build colorful doors and place them in front of rocks where they believe elves live."

"Elves like in Santa's workshop?" Tony asks.

"Not exactly," Ms. Frogbottom explains. "In Iceland elves are believed to live a lot like people. They have families and regular jobs. For instance, some are believed to be fishermen and farmers."

Sofia is looking at her tablet again. "It says here that elves get really angry when their houses are disturbed," she reads. "And when they get mad, they play tricks on people."

"I like elves already," Olivia says with a big grin.

Sofia shakes her head. "Their tricks aren't for laughs. Elves use magical powers to do evil things, like break down machinery, or make people sick. Elves can cause bad weather or shut off electricity for days at a time. In Iceland, doing something to upset elves is considered *very* bad luck."

"Come on, Sofia," I say.

"I'm just telling you what it says in this article," Sofia explains. "A lot of people in Iceland consider the elves' feelings in everything they do. They don't want to make the elves angry."

"What do you mean?" Oliver asks.

Sofia scrolls down a little farther on her tablet. "A few years ago the government wanted to build a road, but a group of elf believers tried to stop them because they were afraid it would disturb an elf village."

"Seriously?" I ask her.

"Yup." Sofia nods as she stares at her

tablet screen. "There are a lot of folktales about elves. That's what they read at the Elfschool."

"Elves go to school?" Tony says.

"The Elfschool is a place where *humans* can go to learn more about elves," Sofia explains. "It's in Iceland's capital city of Reykjavík."

"No thanks," I tell her. "Going to Left Turn Alleyway Elementary is plenty for me. I don't need more school."

Oops. I almost forgot that Ms. Frogbottom is standing next to me. "I mean—I like school," I stammer nervously. "We learn lots of interesting things. I just need time for after-school sports and . . ."

Ms. Frogbottom laughs. "It's okay. Don't

worry. We're not going to the Elfschool. The whole point of a field trip is to experience the world *outside* of school. I like when you use your five senses to learn."

"Emma!" Olivia exclaims. "There's something in your hair." Olivia moves a little closer. "I think it's a worm!"

"It can't be," Sofia assures Emma. "It's too cold for worms to be aboveground."

But Emma can't hear what Sofia is saying. She's too busy jumping around and shouting, "Get it off! Get it off!"

"Relax. I've got it." Olivia holds up a long brown worm . . . *and pops it into her mouth.*

"Mmmm . . . gooey," Olivia says as she chews the worm.

Emma looks like she's about to throw up.

"Tastes like root beer," Olivia tells us.

Now I get it. "That was a gummy worm, wasn't it?"

Olivia giggles and smiles at Emma. "Gotcha!"

Emma glares. She opens her mouth to yell at Olivia, but she doesn't get the chance, because at just that moment Ms. Frogbottom opens her Magic Map. She points to a new spot in Iceland.

"And we're off!" I shout as a white light flashes all around us. My body feels weightless, and I think my feet have just left the ground.

It's like I'm flying in space. And then . . .

3

"SOMETHING WET AND COLD IS DRIPPING on me," I announce after we land at a . . .

Or is it *on* a . . . ?

Or *in* a . . . ?

I have no idea where the Magic Map has taken us this time. All I know is that it's completely dark and cold, and something is definitely dripping from above.

"There's often a bit of water inside a

lava tube," Ms. Frogbottom explains. "It's nothing to worry about."

Now I know where we are. We're inside a lava tube.

Whatever a lava tube is.

"Have I mentioned that I don't like being in the dark?" Tony remarks.

Ms. Frogbottom pulls a giant-size lantern from her backpack. Then she hands us each a plastic helmet with a little light on it. "These will help you find your way through the cave."

Okay, so now I know that a lava tube is a kind of cave.

"Are all the walls made from lava?" Oliver asks.

"Yes," Ms. Frogbottom answers. "At

one time this lava tube, which is called Vidgelmir cave, was completely sealed. There was no way to enter. But the roof of the lava tube collapsed in two places. Now there's a way for people to climb in and out."

Or you can arrive by Magic Map, I think. *Like we did.*

"Collapsed?" Tony repeats. "You mean this roof could fall on us at any minute?"

"Well, technically that's true," Ms. Frogbottom admits. "But it's been decades since anything like that has happened. I think we're safe."

"Y-y-you *think*?" Tony gulps.

"Will we find stalactites in this cave?" Sofia asks Ms. Frogbottom.

"Oh yes," Ms. Frogbottom replies. "And stalagmites too."

"Wow!" Sofia sounds really excited.

I have no idea what Sofia and Ms. Frogbottom are talking about. It's like they're speaking in a secret code that only teachers and class brains understand.

"Follow me," Ms. Frogbottom says as she leads us along the wooden walkway that's been built in the center of the lava tube.

The farther we walk, the more the colors of the cave seem to change. When we started, the walls were basically black lava. But now I'm seeing some spots that are bright orange, and other areas where the wall gives off a purplish-blue glow.

"Careful of those icicles overhead, Aiden!" Olivia says with a giggle.

I can't believe Olivia's playing that same trick on me. But we're not in the middle of a game of tag now. It can't hurt me to stop and look up at the top of the cave.

"Wowza!" I exclaim. "Those are some massive icicles."

Sofia shakes her head. "Those are stalactites. They look like icicles, but they are actually made from calcium deposits, not water."

"Look at the gold, turquoise, and purple!" Emma exclaims. "It's like nature has splattered paint all over."

"In a way it has," Ms. Frogbottom tells

her. "Each of those colors is formed by a different mineral in the rocks."

"Those stalagmites on the ground look like they're glowing," Sofia says, pointing to what looks like a group of upside-down bluish-white icicles springing up from the ground.

"That glow is the reflection from our lights," Ms. Frogbottom explains. "Now come along. There's so much to see in this cave."

My classmates and I walk along in silence. No one is talking. We're too focused on the stalactites and stalagmites around us. All I hear is the sound of our footsteps until . . .

Hee-hee-hee-hee.

"Hey, did you guys hear something?" I ask my classmates.

Everyone stands still, listening.

"Nope," Emma says finally. And she's right. The *hee-hee-hee*-ing has stopped. But that doesn't mean it didn't happen.

"I don't think we're alone in here," I say. But no one pays attention to me.

Oliver points to some markings on the side of the cave. "Look at those rocks. Don't they look like faces?"

I stare at the cave wall. I guess if I squint, I can kind of see the outline of two human faces, with pointy ears.

"That looks like an elf!" Olivia exclaims excitedly. "Do you think there are elves living in here?"

"I hope not," Tony answers nervously. "Those elves sounded awful. I wouldn't want to be the one to make them angry."

"What reason would they have to be angry?" Olivia asks him. "We're just walking."

"Who knows? Maybe they don't like us coming close to where they live," Tony suggests.

"There's no such thing as elves," Sofia assures Tony. "Those are only stories the ancient Vikings brought to Iceland."

What Sofia is saying makes sense. It's hard to believe that there's really a whole civilization of people living in tiny villages in the rocks of Iceland. And yet . . .

Hee-hee-hee.

I'm absolutely sure I heard someone laughing this time.

We walk a little farther, and I see sunlight in the distance. We've reached the end of this lava tunnel.

"We made it!" Tony shouts a minute later as we exit the cave into the sunlight.

For once I'm as relieved as Tony. As cool as it was to be inside a tube of lava from an ancient volcano, there was definitely something creepy going on in there.

But now that's all behind us. We made it out of the tunnel fine. . . .

No. Wait. We haven't made it out fine. *Someone is missing.* Which is not unusual for our class. Even though we're supposed to stay together, somebody *always* seems to go missing on our field trips.

"Where's Olivia?" I ask Oliver.

Oliver looks around. "She was behind me a minute ago."

"She's not now," I reply.

"We gotta find her," Oliver insists. "Before Ms. Frogbottom notices she's missing."

Ms. Frogbottom is the least of Olivia's problems. I really think there's someone in that cave. And if they've got Olivia . . .

"Wait up, you guys!" Olivia shouts from inside the tunnel.

I turn around in time to see her shove something into her pocket. It looks like a black rock—just like the lava we've been seeing here in Iceland.

Except it couldn't be Icelandic lava. Olivia knows Ms. Frogbottom's field trip rule. We're not allowed to bring home souvenirs. Ms. Frogbottom believes the things we discover on our field trips should stay in the countries they come from. Olivia wouldn't break one of Ms. Frogbottom's rules on purpose.

RUMBLE. GRUMBLE.

Suddenly I hear a loud noise. Like a volcano erupting.

Only, the sounds aren't coming from a volcano. They're coming from my stomach. "Is anybody else hungry?" I ask.

My classmates all start to laugh. Even Ms. Frogbottom chuckles a little. And I know why. It's because I'm always hungry.

Especially when we're on a field trip. Knowing that there are new and different foods to try always sets my stomach growling.

"I'm sure it's time to eat," I tell my classmates. "My stomach is never wrong."

"I know a wonderful restaurant," Ms. Frogbottom tells me. "But it's too far to walk to from here."

That's no big deal. Ms. Frogbottom can just pull out her map, and we'll be there in a jiffy.

But Ms. Frogbottom doesn't reach into her backpack. Instead she whips off one of her gloves, sticks two fingers into her mouth, and lets out a loud whistle.

A moment later a huge sled, pulled by three giant reindeer, arrives beside us.

Ms. Frogbottom walks over to the driver of the sleigh and says something to him. The driver nods, and then our teacher calls out to us.

"Hop onto the sleigh," she says. "The reindeer will take us where we need to go."

"Do these reindeer fly?" Tony asks nervously as he climbs onto the sleigh. "You know, like Santa's reindeer?"

The twins giggle. But I don't. Because I was kind of wondering the same thing. I would never say it out loud, though, because believing in Santa is, well . . .

FROGBOTTOM FACT

★ Reindeer are not native to Iceland. They were brought to the island from Norway in the 1700s.

you know . . . kind of embarrassing. And yet, since I've had Ms. Frogbottom for a teacher, I've met up with a whole lot of folks I'd never have believed in before.

"We'll be on solid ground the whole time," Ms. Frogbottom assures Tony. "Mr. Brandari here will make sure of it."

I sit on the sleigh and stick my hands into my pockets—for extra warmth. And that's when I realize that something's missing.

"My lucky Stan 'Slugger' Sampson baseball card!" I shout. "It fell out of my pocket."

"Are you sure you had it with you?" Oliver asks me.

"It's always in this pocket," I tell him. "I keep it zipped in there. Except, my pocket zipper was open. I *never* leave that pocket open—unless I have my hand in it."

"I'm afraid we don't have time to go back to look for your card now, Aiden," Ms. Frogbottom tells me.

I'm so bummed, I've lost my appetite. Well, almost, anyway. I could never lose my appetite *completely*.

The sleigh driver cracks the reins, and

the reindeer take off along the icy road at top speed. It's fast and exciting. But all I can think about is how many packs of baseball cards I had to go through to get that Stan "Slugger" Sampson card.

And then I hear it again. *Hee-hee-hee-hee.*

4

WHOOSH!

You'd think pulling a whole class of kids and their teacher on a sleigh would slow these reindeer down. But you'd be wrong. We're *zooming* our way to the restaurant.

The faster we go, the harder the wind smacks me in the face. I have my scarf pulled to the top of my nose, and my hood pulled over my forehead. All you can see are my eyes.

"Darn it!" Sofia exclaims suddenly. "I lost my strawberry lip balm. This wind is really chapping my lips."

"You lost the lip balm *I* gave you?" Emma asks.

"I'm sorry," Sofia apologizes. "It must have fallen out of my pocket. I know I had it when we were in the lava tunnel."

Hmmm. . . . Sofia had something in her pocket, and now it's gone. I had something in my pocket, and now *it's* gone. I'm sensing a pattern here.

I wonder if the thing I saw Olivia put into her pocket is still there. I can't ask without sounding like I'm accusing her of taking a piece of lava out of the cave. I won't do that unless I'm actually sure that's what she did. So I'll just sit here, quietly inhaling the wool from the scarf I tied around my mouth and nose.

"Whoa!" Mr. Brandari pulls on the reins. Almost immediately the reindeer come to a full stop.

But we're not in front of a restaurant. There's nothing but big black rocks here.

"We'll be at the restaurant in a few minutes," Ms. Frogbottom explains. "First Mr. Brandari wants to show you Dimmuborgir."

I don't know exactly what Dimmuborgir is, but I'm pretty sure it's not going to fill anyone's stomach.

"'*Dimmuborgir*' means 'black fortress,'" Mr. Brandari tells us. "You see those large dark pillars of rock up there? They may look like they were made by an erupting volcano, but . . ."

I roll my eyes. That's *exactly* what they look like. Just like all the other lava rocks we've seen. Nothing special. So why are we out here in the cold when we could be in a nice warm restaurant?

"According to Icelandic legends, those rocks were once trolls," Mr. Brandari continues. "A type of hidden supernatural folk."

"Like elves?" Emma asks.

"Trolls are much meaner and angrier

FROGBOTTOM FACT

★ Iceland is home to more than a hundred volcanoes. It is believed that about thirty are active.

than elves," Mr. Brandari replies. "They're also huge—taller than humans."

Considering that elves can cause bad weather or make people sick, I can't imagine how much meaner trolls could be.

"Trolls come out in the darkness to capture children who misbehave," Mr. Brandari tells us. "They cook the children up and eat them for dinner!"

We look at one another. That does sound pretty scary. But no scarier than some of the things we've heard before.

"Everywhere we go there's someone who wants to eat kids," Tony says. "Remember the kelpies in Scotland? They were kid-eaters. So were the capcauns in Romania. Aren't there any monsters anywhere that eat *adults*?"

I have no idea. All I know is that all this talk about eating is making me hungrier.

"You said those rocks were once trolls," Sofia reminds Mr. Brandari. "What happened to them?"

"Trolls love parties," Mr. Brandari explains. "The louder and crazier the better. They love music and dancing. There aren't any rules about how wild a troll party can get—except one."

"What's that?" Emma asks.

"Trolls have to be back in their caves before sunrise. Otherwise they'll turn to stone."

I think I see where Mr. Brandari is going with this.

"One night the local trolls threw a party. They invited trolls from all over Iceland to join the fun. There was singing and dancing and plenty of food to eat," Mr. Brandari continues.

"I could go for some of that food right now," I whisper to Oliver. My appetite has come back.

Ms. Frogbottom shoots me a look and puts her finger to her lips. Boy, does she have good ears.

"The trolls were having such a wonderful time that they didn't notice the sun coming up on the horizon," Mr. Brandari explains. "Before any of them knew what was happening, the trolls had turned to stone. If we were to walk around this area, we'd see many of those stone trolls."

"We're not going to do that, are we?" Tony asks Mr. Brandari. "I don't think I could walk very far. My feet are freezing. Especially the right foot. Which is kind of wei—" Tony stops himself before finishing the word.

We're not supposed to say "weird"

when we're on field trips. It's one of Ms. Frogbottom's rules.

"I mean *unusual*," Tony finishes.

That *is* unusual. But no more than anything else that's been happening around here.

Hee-hee-hee....

See what I mean?

"You guys heard that, right?" I say.

"I definitely heard something," Sofia agrees.

Finally.

"It sounds like the wind blowing through the trees," Sofia continues.

Grrr. It's *not* the wind. Someone is laughing at us. I'm sure of it. I just can't figure out who it is.

"I'M GLAD TO BE INSIDE," EMMA SAYS AS she hangs her jacket on a hook.

We've just arrived at the restaurant, and we're busy taking off our coats, hats, scarves, and gloves in the cloakroom.

"It's going to take a long time to warm up," I say. "My cheeks feel like blocks of ice."

"I'm keeping my jacket on while I eat," Olivia says. She looks at Ms. Frogbottom.

"That's okay, right? I'm really cold."

Ms. Frogbottom takes off her Viking helmet and places it back in her pack. "You can wear your jacket if you like, but personally I'm feeling quite warm," she replies. Then she walks over and says something to a man in a thick gray sweater who is standing behind a small podium.

"I'm definitely still cold," Olivia says as she shoves her hands into her jacket pockets.

I wonder if Olivia is wearing her jacket because she's really cold, or because she wants to keep her hand on whatever's hidden in her pocket.

"Hey! Where'd my sock go?" Tony exclaims as he slips off his boots to try to straighten both his socks. But one is missing. He wiggles the toes on his bare right foot.

"Maybe it's stuck inside the boot," Sofia suggests.

Tony reaches into his boot. "Nope. I definitely put on both socks this morning. No matter how late I might be running, I would never put on only one sock."

"At least now you know why one foot was warmer than the other," I tell him.

Tony frowns as he sticks his sockless foot back into his boot.

"Come along, everyone," Ms. Frogbottom calls to us. "Our table is ready. Let's head into the dining room."

We follow the man in the gray sweater

past the tables of other diners toward a small corner near the fireplace, where a round table has been set for us. It's made of slats of old wood—kind of like a picnic table. Almost everything in this room is made of wood—the chairs, the walls, even the ceiling. I feel like I'm in a log cabin. When I look up, I see a big chandelier made from what look like reindeer antlers.

I hurry to get the chair closest to the fireplace. I'm still feeling the chill from that sleigh ride.

"Tony, sit next to me," Olivia calls from the other side of the table.

That's strange. It's not like Olivia and Tony are friends or anything.

Tony shrugs and heads over to the empty chair next to her. The minute he sits down, he lets out a really loud noise. Kind of like a burp—but from his other end.

Everyone in the dining room turns to stare at Tony. One man chuckles really loudly.

Tony turns beet red. "I didn't," he insists. "It wasn't me. I . . ."

Olivia starts laughing. "For a mini whoopee cushion, that thing sure is loud!"

"Whoopee cushion?" Tony stands up and lifts a small, red balloon-like object from his chair. He throws it onto the table and glares at Olivia. "Why did you do that?"

"Because . . . it's . . . funny!" Olivia can barely get the words out, she's laughing so hard.

Ms. Frogbottom is *not* laughing. "There is a time and place for practical jokes," she says. "This isn't it. Please apologize."

Olivia stops laughing. "Sorry, Tony," she mumbles as she tucks the whoopee cushion into her jacket pocket.

Two waitresses come toward us, each carrying a tray of food.

"Yuck! What's this?" Oliver exclaims as they place dishes of smelly white squares in front of us.

"Oliver!" Ms. Frogbottom scolds.

"Sorry. I mean, what have you served us?" he asks more politely.

"*Hákarl*," one waitress replies. "Dried shark meat."

A terrible smell wafts up toward my

FROGBOTTOM FACTS

★ Most traditional Icelandic dishes have their roots in ancient Scandinavian recipes that were brought by the Vikings in the ninth and tenth centuries.
★ Icelandic meals often include fish, dairy, lamb, potatoes, and bread.

nose, kind of like a combination of vinegar and ammonia. Usually I'll try anything. But *this*? No way. It stinks too badly to eat.

Ms. Frogbottom seems to be enjoying the shark meat, though. "*Hákarl* takes a long time to prepare," she tells us. "It's buried in the sand for two to three months. Then it's cut into pieces and hung to dry. It's considered quite a delicacy here."

Nothing Ms. Frogbottom says is going to convince me—or any of my classmates—to give the *hákarl* a try. Our plates are untouched when the waitresses come to take them away and serve the next course.

"This is lamb soup," a waitress says as she places a big bowl of steaming-hot soup in front of me. "Our specialty."

That's more like it! The soup smells delicious. The broth is filled with hunks of meat as well as thick slices of carrots and other vegetables.

I take a giant slurp. "Yum!" I exclaim. "Soup is exactly what I needed."

"I love hot soup on cold days," Emma agrees—which is kind of amazing, since Emma and I rarely agree on anything.

A little while later the waitresses clear away our empty bowls and return with dessert. We're each given a hunk of fried dough with a hole in the middle. It almost looks like a doughnut, except instead of being round, the pastry is diamond-shaped.

"You are each getting a *kleina* as a

treat," one of the waitresses tells us.

I take a bite of the hot fried dough. It's sweet and buttery, with just enough powdered sugar on top to leave white spots on everyone's lips. The *kleina* is pretty much perfect. In fact, the only thing wrong with this treat is that there isn't enough of it.

"Thank you so much," Ms. Frogbottom tells the waitresses as she pays the bill. "This meal was delicious. But we have to hurry if we're going to have time for the geothermal baths."

We follow our teacher back to the cloakroom and start putting on our layers and layers of clothing.

Ms. Frogbottom reaches into her backpack. A strange look comes over her face.

"It has to be here somewhere," she mutters.

"What has to be there?" I ask her.

"My map," Ms. Frogbottom replies. "I'm sure I put it in my backpack." She starts digging through her pack.

We watch as our teacher yanks out her Viking hat, a snorkel, a French horn, her giant lantern, a tennis racket, two boxes of frozen waffles, an artist's palette, a rubber duckie, the six plastic helmets with lights attached, a jar of dill pickles, and an unwrapped mint covered in lint.

Believe it or not, none of that surprises me.

"The map's not here," Ms. Frogbottom says finally.

We all turn and stare at Olivia.

"I didn't take it," she assures us. "Practical jokes are supposed to be funny. There's nothing funny about a missing Magic Map."

She's not kidding. That map is how we traveled to Iceland.

It's also supposed to be our transportation back.

Which makes me wonder. Without that map, how are we ever going to get home?

"UH-OH," EMMA SAYS AS WE STEP OUTSIDE.

I know what she means. It's getting dark. Which is a big problem, because we're supposed to be back at school before dismissal. If it's already dark, we're late.

"My mom's gonna be so worried," Tony says.

"We have plenty of time before we have to be back," Ms. Frogbottom assures us. "It's earlier than you think. Iceland is way up near the Arctic Circle. This time of year, Iceland is so far from the sun, it only gets about four hours of daylight. Iceland makes up for those short winter days in the summer, when the sun sometimes doesn't set till midnight."

"I'm really glad we're not late." Tony sounds very relieved. But I don't know why. The Magic Map is still missing. And without that, we're definitely not getting home by dismissal. Which is a real bummer. I was planning on spending the whole afternoon finishing my new mystery book.

Wait. That's it! I have an idea for how we can find the Magic Map.

"Ms. Frogbottom, where was the last

place you actually saw the map?" I ask, trying to sound like one of the detectives in the mystery books I've read.

"When we arrived in the lava cave," my teacher responds. "I put it in my backpack."

"We need to go back there," I tell her. "We should return to the scene of the crime."

"What crime?" Oliver asks me.

"This is the Case of the Missing Map," I reply. "Someone took that map. And I'll bet they did it before we left for the restaurant."

"What makes you think that?" Tony wonders.

"Because other things disappeared at

that lava cave too," I reply. "My baseball card, Sofia's lip balm—"

"That *I* gave her," Emma reminds us. "Because she's my friend."

"I said I was sorry," Sofia insists.

"Tony's sock disappeared there too," I continue. "And Ms. Frogbottom's map. I think we ran into a thief near the tunnel."

"Or the map could have fallen out of the backpack, and our pockets may have been open by mistake," Sofia points out.

"That makes more sense," Emma agrees.

"Maybe. But it doesn't explain how my sock disappeared," Tony points out.

"You probably just forgot to put it on," Sofia tells him.

"I did not," Tony insists.

"Going back to the cave is a good idea," Ms. Frogbottom says, interrupting their argument. "I'll call for a van. The reindeer sleigh would be too slow if we want to get there in time to catch a thief," she says.

Ahem. Sofia clears her throat.

"Or find the map where it fell out of my backpack," Ms. Frogbottom adds, looking at Sofia. Our teacher pulls her phone from her pocket and makes a call.

A few minutes later a van pulls up beside us, and we pile in.

As we drive off into the darkness, I start to worry. Ms. Frogbottom sounds like she thinks my plan will work and we will get the Magic Map back. But what if whoever took the map is gone? What if they've traveled someplace far away, and taken our map with them? There are a lot of things that can go wrong with this plan.

Thump. Bump. Flump.

Uh-oh.

Our van comes to a quick stop. It's dark out, but the headlights are bright. I can see that we are definitely not back at Vidgelmir cave.

Ms. Frogbottom says something to our driver, who answers her in Icelandic.

I didn't know that my teacher speaks Icelandic. But she must, because Ms. Frogbottom nods and then tells us, "It's a flat tire. We have to get out so the driver can fix things."

See what I mean about things that could go wrong?

"How long will that take?" Tony asks nervously.

"Not long." For some reason Ms. Frogbottom doesn't seem stressed about this. "In the meantime, I want to show you all something amazing," she adds.

As we get out of the van, Ms. Frogbottom pulls her lantern out of her backpack and starts walking. My classmates and I follow close behind. We pass a few bare trees, a cave, and a pile of rocks. None of that seems too "amazing," but then . . .

WHOOSH!

Suddenly a blast of steaming water bursts from the ground. It shoots into the

air like a rocket.
A moment later
it disappears.

"That's an
eruption of the
Strokkur geyser,"
Ms. Frogbottom
tells us. "We are
standing near
one of the
most famous
tourist sites in
Iceland."

"I've never
seen anything
like it," I say.

"Wait awhile,

and you'll see it again," Ms. Frogbottom tells me. "The Strokkur geyser erupts every fifteen minutes. You can time it if you like. It's very reliable."

Ms. Frogbottom hands me her light. "Here, Aiden," she says. "You be the lantern monitor. I'm going to see if I can help our van driver with that tire change."

"Olivia, are you wearing your watch?" Oliver asks as our teacher heads back toward the van.

Olivia doesn't answer.

FROGBOTTOM FACT

★ The English word "geyser" comes from the name of an Icelandic geyser called "Geysir." It was named after the Old Norse word *geysa*, which means "to rush forth."

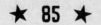

"Olivia?" Oliver repeats. He looks around for his sister. But she's gone.

Again.

"Where'd Olivia go?" Oliver wonders.

"She probably stopped to fix her shoelaces again," Emma says. "She needs to learn to tie a double knot."

I don't see Olivia anywhere. Not near the trees. Or beside the rocks. Or outside the cave. Although . . .

"Hey! Isn't that Olivia's scarf?" I ask, pointing the lantern toward a wool scarf outside the cave. That's when I spy three sets of footprints going into the cave. One set is kid-size. But the other two sets of prints are huge.

Monstrously huge.

I remember what the sleigh driver told us about trolls. They're bigger than humans, which would probably mean that they have bigger feet, too.

He also said that trolls come out at night and capture children who mis-behave. And Olivia's been pulling those mean practical jokes all day long.

I shoot Oliver a look. "Now, don't get

upset," I urge, trying to sound calm. "But I think your sister may have been captured by trolls. Look at these three sets of footprints." I shine the lantern toward the opening of the cave.

Oliver stares at the prints and then glares at me. "You think my sister has been kidnapped by kid-eating monsters, but you don't think I should be upset?"

Okay, maybe that was a dumb thing to say.

"Do *you* think trolls took Olivia?" Emma asks Sofia.

Grrr. Why does Emma always have to doubt me? Can't I be right once in a while?

Sofia shrugs. "I don't believe in trolls

or elves. I truly think they're just characters in old folktales."

"You said the same thing about the
Loch Ness monster, vampires, and mum-
mies that have come back to life," I remind
her. "You were wrong every time."

"I like facts," Sofia insists. "And seeing
things with my own eyes. Have you seen a
real troll? Or a real elf?"

She's got me there.

"Whether there are trolls or not, Olivia
is missing," Emma says. "So what do we
do now?"

Sofia thinks. "I don't know," she admits.

"What do you mean, you don't know?"
Oliver asks her. "You're the class brain.
You *have* to know."

"I don't like it when you call me 'class brain,'" Sofia replies. "And I really have no idea how to find Olivia."

I hope Sofia is right about there not being trolls.

I hope Olivia isn't really in that cave.

I hope she's just hiding and playing another joke on us. Because if Olivia's in there with trolls, she's a goner. I can imagine the trolls all dancing around inside that cave, celebrating the fact that they've captured their next meal. . . .

Suddenly a smile forms on my face. I know *exactly* what we need to do.

"Let's party!" I exclaim.

7

"MY SISTER IS BEING HELD CAPTIVE BY
hungry trolls, and you want to throw a
party?" Oliver asks me.

"Yup."

"You must be really angry that Olivia
ruined that game of tag," Tony says.

"This has nothing to do with tag," I
assure him.

"I think a party is a great idea," Emma
says.

"Have you gone nuts too?" Oliver asks her.

"Nope," Emma assures him. "I know why Aiden wants to throw a party. He wants to lure the trolls out of their cave. Remember, Mr. Brandari told us that trolls love a party."

"Exactly," I say. "Once the trolls come out, we can distract them. Then Olivia will be free to escape."

Oliver doesn't look so sure. "What if the trolls *don't* come out?"

"They will," I assure him.

"There are five of us," Oliver reminds me. "And only two sets of troll footprints. Which means there are more of us than them. We could just go in there and rescue Olivia."

"No way," Tony says, shaking his head.

"If we go in there, we could all get trapped. Then the trolls would have a whole *buffet* of kids for dinner!"

KABLOOM!

Suddenly I hear a loud explosion coming from behind us. "What was that?" I exclaim nervously.

Sofia and Emma start to laugh.

"It was the geyser," Sofia tells me. "Ms. Frogbottom told us it would explode again, remember?"

"Oh yeah, right," I say. I can feel my cheeks getting hot with embarrassment. "It just, um, surprised me. Anyway, about my party idea . . ."

Oliver looks at Sofia. "You sure you don't have any plan at all?"

Sofia shakes her head.

"So let's give mine a try," I say. "It's worth a shot, anyway."

Oliver can't argue with that. "Okay," he says. "But this had better work."

"It will," I insist. "Let's get this party started. Sofia, play some dance music on your tablet."

Sofia clicks on an app, and a song by Lala Radala, Emma's favorite singer, begins to play.

"Now, everybody, act like you're having a good time!" I tell my classmates.

Emma and Sofia start dancing and singing along with the music.

"Woo-hoo!" Tony shouts.

"I love a good PARTY!" I cheer. I start

jumping up and down like a pogo stick.

"PARTY! PARTY! PARTY!" Tony, Sofia, and Emma join in.

Oliver isn't dancing or cheering. He's standing there, staring at the mouth of the cave.

Where nothing is happening. Not even a troll *toe* has poked its way out.

"We're wasting time," Oliver says. "They might be eating already. Do you think they'll cook Olivia, or just bite into her raw leg?"

I don't have an answer. It's too disgusting to think about.

"I was sure that the minute those trolls heard the word 'party,' they'd come running," I say.

Sofia thinks for a minute. "I'm not saying there's such a thing as trolls," she tells us. "But if they *did* exist here, they'd probably speak Icelandic."

She searches for something on her tablet. Then she shouts out something that sounds sort of like "Ow di-jamma!"

We all stare at her.

"'*Að djamma*' means 'to party' in Icelandic," Sofia explains.

"*Að djamma!*" I scream over the music.

"*Að djamma!*" Emma, Tony, and Oliver echo.

Ms. Frogbottom looks over at us from the van. She waves and smiles.

She must think we're celebrating the shooting geyser behind us.

But we don't have anything to cele-brate. The trolls are not coming out.

"I guess that settles it," Sofia says. "There are no such things as trolls."

Ugh. My plan is a failure. And I was so sure the trolls would come out to party, like they did in that story the sleigh driver told us.

Maybe trolls only party with other trolls. Which means they won't come out to dance with us.

Olivia has no way of escaping. If she's even in there.

I bury my head in my hands. I feel like a total failure. Until suddenly I hear Emma shouting.

"There they are!" she cries out. "The

trolls! They're joining the party."

I look up. Sure enough, I see two trolls emerging from the cave.

"Keep dancing!" I tell my classmates. *"Að djamma! Að djamma!"*

My stomach starts to flip-flop at the sight of the trolls. They are really ugly. Their hair looks like straw, and their noses are covered with giant warts. Their eyes bulge from their heads, and there is so much dirt coming out of their ears that you could grow potatoes in there. They're also huge. And the way they stomp those big feet of theirs makes the ground beneath us shake like an earthquake. If my plan doesn't work and they try to capture us, I'm not so sure the five

of us could take them. They're too big.

My friends must be thinking the same thing. They've stopped dancing and cheering. They're just standing there, staring at the giant trolls.

It looks like the party is over.

I can't let that happen. Our only chance is to lure those trolls far enough from their cave for Olivia to make her escape.

I start shouting more loudly and dancing more crazily. *"Að djamma!"*

My friends get the message and join in. *"Að djamma! Að djamma!"*

The creepy-looking trolls sure know how to dance. They swivel their hips and kick their legs. They link elbows and twirl in a circle. They're having a great time.

Now's my chance. I boogie my way over to the mouth of the cave and start shouting, "Olivia! Run! Now!"

I wait for Olivia to come running. But she doesn't. She's nowhere in sight.

Suddenly I'm not in a partying mood. Maybe Olivia isn't in there after all. Which means we're out here dancing like crazy people with a pair of hideous, huge kid-eating trolls for no reason.

No. Wait. There *is* someone still in the cave. I see a head peeking out. And it's not a big, wart-covered troll head either. It's a kid-size head.

Olivia's head!

Olivia looks around suspiciously. I bet she's thinking this could be a troll trick.

"Run, Olivia!" I shout as loudly as I can. "Hurry!"

This time, Olivia listens. She races out of the cave so fast, it's like she's flying. She heads straight for Ms. Frogbottom and the van.

"Come on, you guys!" I shout over the music. I'm lucky the trolls have no idea what I'm saying, because you can bet they'd be plenty mad.

The trolls are holding hands and spinning. My friends and I are dancing too— away from the cave and toward the van.

"Excellent. You're all here," Ms. Frogbottom tells us. "The tire is fixed. We can get on our way."

Sounds good! I hurry into the van, with

my classmates right behind me. Ms. Frog-bottom sits down in the front seat next to the driver. He turns on the engine, and we're off.

Not two seconds later Olivia exclaims, "Wait! Stop!"

"What now?" I ask her.

"I lost my scarf."

"Forget it," I tell her.

"But it's my favorite," Olivia insists.

"Do you really want to go back to the troll cave?" Tony points toward the trolls, who have stopped dancing and are staring menacingly at our van. "Because that's where your scarf is."

Olivia slumps down in her seat. "Never mind," she grumbles.

"What was it like in there, anyway?" Oliver asks her.

"Dark," Olivia tells him. "They only had two candles to light the whole place. And it smelled awful. Like those trolls hadn't washed in years."

"They didn't look very clean," Emma agrees.

"The scariest thing was this giant pot in the middle of the cave," Olivia continues. "They were boiling water—to cook *me*."

I smile proudly. It was my idea that saved Olivia from being boiled like a lobster. Plus, I was able to give Sofia absolute proof that trolls exist. Which means I was right, and the class brain was wrong.

I can be a smart kid when I want to be.

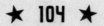

That's why I'm feeling really confident that we'll find the Magic Map and my lucky Stan "Slugger" Sampson baseball card back at the lava tube.

I'm starting to relax. But then . . .

"What is that?" Emma shouts suddenly.

I look out the window. Green and white streaks are flashing wildly in the sky.

"Space aliens!" Tony exclaims.

Sparks of purple join the green and white streaks. Tony could be right. I've never seen anything like those lights.

Probably because I've never seen a spaceship before.

"We've got to get someplace safe!" I urge. "We can't let space creatures capture us and take us to their alien planet.

We don't have the Magic Map to bring us back to Earth anymore."

My teacher smiles and claps her hands. "How lucky!" she exclaims.

Lucky? To be captured by space aliens? Ms. Frogbottom has flipped her lid.

Apparently so has Sofia, because she's grinning from ear to ear. "The aurora borealis!" she cheers. "I've always wanted to see this."

"Aurora," Emma repeats. "That's a great name. From now on I want all of you to call me 'Aurora.'"

Sofia giggles. "Until tomorrow, when you'll want us to call you something else."

Emma shrugs. "Probably."

"Those are the northern lights," Ms.

Frogbottom explains. "Also known as the aurora borealis. You can see them clearly during some of Iceland's dark nights."

"So they aren't space aliens who have come to take us to their leader?" Tony asks.

Ms. Frogbottom shakes her head. "These are natural electrical occurrences in the sky. Think of them as nature's light show."

"The lights are dancing!" Emma squeals. She begins to dance in her seat. At least I *think* that's what she's doing.

FROGBOTTOM FACTS

★ Auroras occur mostly near the North and South Poles.

★ No two displays of the northern lights are ever the same. The patterns are always different.

Mostly she's waving her hands in circles.

I know that Ms. Frogbottom says we can't use the word "weird" when we're on field trips. But sometimes Emma can be very . . . well . . . you know.

Still, like I said, I'm a smart kid. Which is why I don't say anything about how Emma is acting. I don't want to have to have a "talk" with Ms. Frogbottom. This field trip has been tough enough already.

Right now I just want to find Ms. Frogbottom's Magic Map and go home.

8

BAM. WHAM. SLAM.

Suddenly the van comes to a hard stop. We all lurch forward in our seats.

I look out the window to see if we've arrived at the lava tunnel. But that's not where we are. We seem to be in the middle of nowhere, with nothing and nobody around.

What's going on?

Has Ms. Frogbottom decided we need

to see some other fantastic site in Iceland? Because honestly, after having my baseball card stolen, losing Olivia at the geyser, and no longer having the Magic Map to get us home, I think I've seen enough.

"Ms. Frogbottom," I say. "Don't you think we'd better get back to the cave before whoever stole the Magic Map takes it somewhere else?"

Ms. Frogbottom says something in Icelandic to our driver.

He replies angrily, shaking his head.

"The motor has stalled," Ms. Frogbottom tells us. "The driver wants us to get out."

"Can't we wait in here until help comes?" Emma asks. "It's cold outside."

Ms. Frogbottom shakes her head. "He's convinced that elves are cursing his van. He thinks it's our fault."

"*Our* fault?" Oliver wonders. "We're just sitting here."

The driver crosses his arms in front of his chest.

"Now what?" Tony asks nervously as we pile out of the van.

My plan to get the map will only work if we return to the cave. "How far away is the lava tube?" I ask Ms. Frogbottom.

"Less than a quarter of a mile."

"We could walk," I suggest.

Ms. Frogbottom holds up her lantern and glances worriedly at her watch. We must be getting close to dismissal time. "I suppose so," she replies. "There's a fork in the road ahead. Let me ask the van driver which way we should go."

Ms. Frogbottom knocks on the van window to get the driver's attention.

But he doesn't open the window. Instead he turns the key in the ignition. *And the engine starts.* Which is odd, since it was stalled just a few minutes ago.

Vroom! Ms. Frogbottom leaps out of the way as the driver takes off, leaving us in the dust.

The cold, dark dust.

"He won't be any help," Ms. Frogbottom says. "But that's okay."

Okay? There is nothing *okay* about this situation.

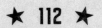

"I have my cell phone," Ms. Frogbottom explains. "I'll use my map app to point us in the right direction." She pulls out her phone and shakes her head. "That's funny."

"Funny *haha* or funny *uh-oh*?" Tony asks her.

"The battery is dead," Ms. Frogbottom replies. "I could have sworn I had at least fifty percent. Sofia, can you program your tablet's GPS to get us back to the cave?"

"Sure." Sofia turns on her tablet. Or at least she *tries* to. "My battery is dead too. I don't get it. I had plenty of power left when we got into the van."

Tony picks nervously at the tip of his mitten. Usually when Tony is scared, he picks at the stringy skin around his fingernails. Right now his mitten is as close as he can get.

I don't blame Tony. Being stuck in the cold on a dark, abandoned road with no Magic Map is terrifying. It could be hours before anyone comes by. We might all freeze to death before then.

This could be the scariest situation we've ever been in during one of Ms. Frogbottom's field trips. And that's saying something.

"Do you think the elves could be causing all this trouble?" Oliver wonders out loud.

"That makes sense," I reply. "The missing items, the broken-down van that started up again the minute we got out, and the mysteriously drained batteries. It sure sounds like we made some elves angry."

"But how?" Tony wonders. "All we've done is visit some places in Iceland. We stared at waterfalls, walked through a lava tunnel . . ."

The lava tunnel. That's it!

"The elves *are* doing this. And I know why!" I exclaim as I shoot Olivia a pointed look. "You know why too."

"Me?" Olivia asks. "What did I do?"

"What's in your pocket?" I demand.

"I don't know what you're talking about."

"Yes, you do," I insist. "I saw you take it."

"What could Olivia have in her pocket that would make elves angry?" Sofia wonders.

"Show her," I tell Olivia.

Olivia gives me a dirty look.

"If you've got something that's keeping us from going home, we have a right to know," Emma insists.

Oliver stares at his sister. "What did you do now?" he asks her.

Olivia frowns. Then, ever so slowly, she pulls a piece of lava from her pocket.

"Olivia!" Ms. Frogbottom scolds. "You know better than to try to bring a souvenir home from a field trip."

Olivia frowns and looks at the ground. "I'm sorry," she apologizes. "There's so much lava everywhere. I didn't think anyone would miss it."

"Well, someone *did* miss it," I tell her. "The elves. That's why we're stuck here. I bet they took Ms. Frogbottom's Magic

Map as payback for you stealing that lava."

Hee-hee-hee....

There's the laughter again. This time it's so loud, *everyone* hears it.

"That's *gotta* be elves," Oliver says.

"Elves are mean," I add. "They're probably laughing because they know that without the map, we're stuck."

Tony frowns and starts picking at his

mitten again. "And there's absolutely nothing we can do about it," he whimpers.

That can't be true. We kids have been through some pretty scary times together on our field trips. We've been menaced in a mummy's tomb, almost captured by a kid-eating kelpie, and vexed by a vicious vampire. Every time, we got out of trouble by jumping into action.

Which is exactly what we have to do now. And I think I know how.

"There's something we can do about it," I assure Tony.

My classmates stare at me.

"We're gonna need those helmets with the lights that we used to go through the lava tunnel," I tell Ms. Frogbottom. "If the elves are here, I bet we're near their houses. We'll need the lights to search their homes for our stolen stuff."

"Are you nuts?" Oliver asks me. "Don't you remember what Sofia read? Elves do terrible things to people who disturb their houses."

"They're *already* doing terrible things to us," I tell Oliver. "We might as well try to find our stuff, take back our Magic Map, and get out of here before it gets worse."

"What do you think, Ms. Frogbottom?" Emma asks.

Our teacher is already reaching into her bag and pulling out the helmets with the little lights on them. "It's worth a try," she replies.

I flick on my helmet light. Now I can see that we're surrounded by rocks with painted doors.

"Let's split up into groups," I tell my classmates. "I'll go to the house with the green door with Tony." I point to the house with the red door. "Olivia and Oliver, you search that one. Emma and Sofia, you guys try the one with the orange door. And Ms. Frogbottom . . ." I stop myself. How do I tell my teacher what to do?

"I'll look near the house with the purple door," Ms. Frogbottom volunteers.

Phew. That made things easier.

As my classmates wander off, I hear them complaining.

"Aiden is so bossy," Olivia tells Oliver.

"He really does think he's king," Emma grouses to Sofia.

I try not to listen as I walk toward the house with the green door, with Tony trailing close behind.

Suddenly the green door bursts open. A small couple comes storming out to meet us. The man has a long white beard and wears a golden crown. The woman wears a smaller crown. They both have pointed ears. And neither one of them looks happy.

"Oh no!" Tony cries. "Elves."

I know exactly how he feels.

"Um . . . you guys . . . ," I say to my class-mates.

"We know," Sofia calls back.

I guess she believes in trolls *and* elves now. Because all of the elf house doors are open. The elves have come out.

These aren't the cute, happy little elves you see in Christmas cartoons. These elves aren't smiling. They're scowling. And they look like they're out for revenge.

The elves were already mad that Olivia had taken that lava. Judging by the expressions on their faces, I have a feeling we've now made them angrier.

It looks like my plan was a *huuuge* mistake.

One of the elves starts spreading

strawberry lip balm across her mouth. She stops just long enough to give Sofia a triumphant glare.

"Give Sofia her lip balm back!" Emma shouts furiously.

The elf smiles and goes back to smearing the strawberry-smelling stuff on her lips.

"That elf is wearing my sock on his ear!" Tony points to the elf outside the house with the purple door. He's wearing Tony's sock like a single earmuff.

Not far from that elf is another one— and he's waving something in the air. Oh no! It's my lucky baseball card. I feel like grabbing it right out of his little elf hand.

But I stop myself. I'm pretty sure that elves really do have dangerous magic powers. How else would they have stolen Tony's sock without him feeling it? And I bet they caused all the trouble with the van and Ms. Frogbottom's phone, too.

Who knows what that elf would do if I reached for my baseball card?

Besides, I'm more worried about the elf in a red cap, standing directly in front of us. He's the one holding Ms. Frogbottom's Magic Map. And right now he's studying the countries on the map.

I look over at my teacher. She seems perfectly calm. But that's got to be an act. Because I'm sure Ms. Frogbottom knows what I've realized: if that elf touches one of those places, he's going to go there.

And he'll take our Magic Map with him.

9

I WISH I KNEW a WaY TO GET MS. Frogbottom's Magic Map back from that elf. But I've racked my brain, and I'm all out of rescue plans. What a lousy time for that to happen.

I'm feeling pretty helpless as I watch the elf men bow and the elf women curtsy to the elves with the crowns.

"They must be the king and queen of the elves," Sofia says.

One of the other elves puts a finger to his lips. I guess you're not supposed to speak in the presence of the king and queen unless you are spoken to.

The same elf smiles at me and bows. The elf with the lip balm curtsies.

"What's that about?" Olivia asks.

"I think *they* think Aiden is our king," Sofia replies.

"Why would they think that?" Olivia wonders.

"Because they heard him bossing us around," Emma replies.

"But Aiden doesn't speak Icelandic," Oliver reminds her. "How would they know he was telling us what to do?"

"You don't have to speak the same

language to know Aiden is bossy," Emma insists. "You can hear it in the tone of his voice. And see it in how he points to show us where to go and what to do."

"I'm not bossy!" I argue. "I just—" I stop myself midsentence. Suddenly I have an idea. "Bow to the king and queen of the elves," I tell my classmates.

"See what I mean?" Emma says. "Bossy."

"Do it," I insist. "Trust me."

Tony shrugs and bows deeply. So does Oliver. Sofia looks at me strangely, but she gives the king and queen a little curtsy. Emma and Olivia do too.

Ms. Frogbottom doesn't move. She keeps her eyes focused on her map, ready to grab it if that elf makes a move with his finger. Which is fine. I'm not going to tell my teacher what to do. She's the one who's *really* in charge. I'm just faking it.

The king of the elves starts talking. Unfortunately, I don't understand a word he's saying.

"What did he say?" Tony asks Ms. Frogbottom.

She shakes her head. "He's talking too fast. I can't understand him."

But I don't need to speak Icelandic to see that the king is angry. And I think I know why, since he keeps pointing at Olivia.

"Show him the lava," I tell her.

"You're not the boss of me," Olivia barks back.

"Show it to him," I insist.

"Fine. But I'm only doing this because of Ms. Frogbottom's rule." Olivia holds out the piece of black rock.

I smile at the king and his elves. Then I point to the lucky baseball card, Sofia's lip balm, Tony's sock, and our Magic Map. I'm trying to show him that we are willing to trade the lava for our belongings.

But the king shakes his head. He's not planning on giving us back anything.

Now what do I do?

Ms. Frogbottom glances down at her watch. We've been in Iceland a long time. We have to get back to school.

And to do that we need the map. More than we need any baseball cards, or lip balm, or even socks.

★ 130 ★

"We're going to have to let them keep our stuff," I tell Sofia and Tony.

"What am I supposed to do with one sock?" Tony asks me.

"Sofia's lips are getting chapped without that lip balm," Emma argues.

"I'll be okay," Sofia assures her.

"Chapped lips are painful," Emma insists. "And besides, I'm sure Aiden will ask for his baseball card back."

"I won't," I promise. "The only thing we really *need* back is the Magic Map. So I'm going to try to trade that piece of lava for the map."

I point to the Magic Map. Then I point to the piece of lava in Olivia's hand.

My heart is really pounding now. If the

king and queen don't take this deal, then we're stuck here.

At night.

In the freezing cold.

Without a working cell phone.

I hold my breath as the king and queen walk over to the elf in the red hat. The king points to the map.

The elf shakes his head.

The queen says something to him in Icelandic.

The elf shakes his head again.

This is not going well. "Please say yes," I whisper quietly under my breath.

The queen whispers something into the elf's pointed ear.

FROGBOTTOM FACT

★ Iceland's entire surface is made of volcanic rock, most of which is basalt.

Lub-dub. Lub-dub. My heart is pounding so hard, I think it's going to burst right out of my rib cage. I have absolutely no idea what's happening.

Finally the elf in the red hat walks over and grabs the piece of lava from Olivia. Then he hands the Magic Map to me and bows—like anyone would, when they meet a king.

That's me. The king of great ideas!

"Here you go, Ms. Frogbottom!" I hand her the Magic Map.

"Thank you, Aiden," she replies.

We all huddle around Ms. Frogbottom. It's definitely time to go. There's not a minute to lose. Not even to say good-bye to the elves. We don't want to give them a chance to change their minds—or steal something else from us.

Ms. Frogbottom touches the map. And . . .

"We're outta here!" I shout.

A white light flashes all around us. My body feels weightless, and I think my feet have just left the ground.

It's like I'm flying in space. And then . . .

10

SPLAT!

A cold, wet snowball slams me in the back of the head.

"I got you, squirt!"

I'd know that voice anywhere. It's my brother, Henry. He's in sixth grade. We walk home from school together. Up until now Henry has acted like he's the king of me. But I'm not letting that happen anymore. I'm a king too.

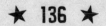

Well, sort of.

Henry has no idea how close he came to walking home by himself today. We got back really late. I barely had time to grab my stuff from the classroom before the bell rang for dismissal.

"Oh yeah?" I reply, scooping up a big ball of snow. I pitch it right at his face. "Take that!"

Bam! The snowball gets Henry between the eyes.

Henry *laughs.* "Good shot, squirt."

I should get mad when Henry calls me "squirt." But I don't. It's a brother thing.

"You do anything fun today?" Henry asks as we walk home.

"We learned about volcanoes and lava," I reply.

"Sounds boring," Henry says.

"Nah. It was cool," I tell him. "So cool that it was *cold.* Freezing even."

Henry gives me a funny look. "What's that supposed to mean?"

"Never mind," I tell him. "You had to be there."

WORDS YOU HEAR ON A FIELD TRIP TO ICELAND

aurora: A natural electrical occurrence that produces streams of lights in the sky, usually near the North and South Poles

basalt: A dark fine-grained volcanic rock

crater: A bowl-shaped hole in the ground

geyser: An underground hot spring in which the water boils, resulting in a shooting stream of hot water into the air

glacier: A slow-moving mass of ice that forms on mountains or near the North and South Poles

 139 ★

hákarl: A national dish of Iceland made of fermented shark meat

kleina: A traditional Icelandic doughnut

lava: Hot, melted rock that erupts from a volcano; also, this rock once it has cooled and hardened

stalactites: Mineral deposits that hang like icicles from the roof or sides of a cave

stalagmites: Mineral deposits that rise up like mounds or columns from the floor of a cave

volcano: A mountain or hill through which lava, rock fragments, vapor, and gas erupt from the earth's crust